The Turtle

and

the

Deep

Blue

Sky

Elizabeth and Eric Zimmer

Fulcrum Publishing

Library of Congress Cataloging-in-Publication Data
Zimmer, Elizabeth (Elizabeth Mary), 1963-
  The turtle and the deep blue sky / written by Elizabeth Zimmer ; illustrated by Eric Zimmer.
     p. cm.
  Summary: When a turtle becomes bored one day and asks to borrow a flamingo's wings, he sets
off a chain reaction that soon has a porcupine wearing a sheep's wool, a fish wearing a peacock's tail
feathers, and other unusual sights.
  ISBN 978-1-55591-597-1 (hardcover)
  [1. Barter--Fiction. 2. Animals--Fiction. 3. Individuality--Fiction. 4. Humorous stories.] I. Zimmer,
Eric, ill. II. Title.
  PZ7.Z61613 Tur 2007
  [Fic]--dc22

                              2007017016

Printed in China by P. Chan and Edward, Inc.
0 9 8 7 6 5 4 3 2 1

Editorial: Haley Berry
Design: Jack Lenzo

 for Fenn

The Turtle
and the
Deep Blue Sky

Elizabeth Zimmer

Illustrations by Eric Zimmer

Once upon a fine day, the animals were
wandering aimlessly here and there.
The turtle, having swum about the pond
all morning, was feeling rather bored.
Not knowing what else to do with himself,
he lay down upon a rock
and gazed up at the deep blue sky.

As the afternoon sun grew warmer,
he began to feel uncomfortably
hot in his heavy green shell.
Longing to feel the cool breeze that was
moving the clouds above, he wondered aloud
if he might borrow a pair of wings from ...

the flamingo.

The flamingo,
having generously lent
the turtle her wings,
was feeling rather silly
and even a bit vulnerable.
If the turtle was going to
borrow her wings,
perhaps she should
borrow some quills from ...

the porcupine.

The porcupine, a very wise
and clever creature indeed,
was delighted at the prospect of bartering
and decided to trade the rest of his quills
for something else. After some thought,
he was convinced he could wiggle
into the wool of ...

the sheep.

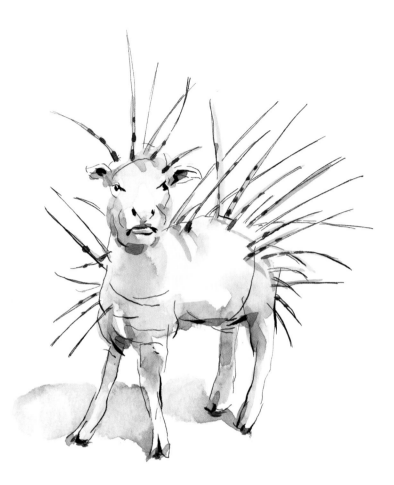

The sheep, though not entirely persuaded
by the practicality of the exchange,
begrudgingly gave up her fluffy fleece.
Feeling prickled and grumpy,
she was inclined to shed the quills
and shimmy into the slick scales of ...

the fish.

As it turns out, the fish had always wanted
to try on some feathers, so he happily gave the
sheep his scales and assured her not to worry,
that he was certain to find a bird willing
to share its finery. Perhaps, he imagined,
even the tail feathers of ...

the peacock.

The peacock,
eager to be relieved of the burden of pride,
was more than happy to oblige.
However, this left him feeling
somewhat exposed and awkward.
The sheepish peacock, embarrassed
at his diminished backside,
was thrilled to come across ...

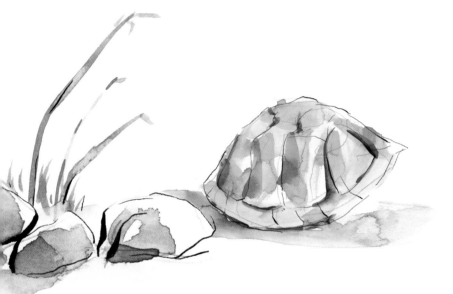

the tortoise shell,
which had been left behind by the turtle,
of course.

Though it was rather heavy, the peacock
was quite pleased with his new shape
and began to strut about.

The turtle,
from his bird's-eye view,
caught sight of his very own shell
swaying to-and-fro in a most unusual way.
Intrigued, he swooped down for a
closer look at his mottled shell.

By now, the peacock
had caught sight of his
very own tail swirling gracefully
behind the fish. Curious, he clunked his way
over to the pond for a better look
at his vibrant plumage.

Meanwhile, the fish was
unexpectedly entranced with
how brilliantly his scales
glittered from afar,
where they adorned the splendid sheep.
He swished to the edge of the pond
to ponder the iridescent reflection of
his gleaming scales.

Unaware that the fish was staring at her,
the sheep was perched on the hillside,
marveling at the versatile uses the porcupine
had invented for her very own wool.
She clambered her way farther up the slope
to peer at the antics of the roly-poly porcupine.

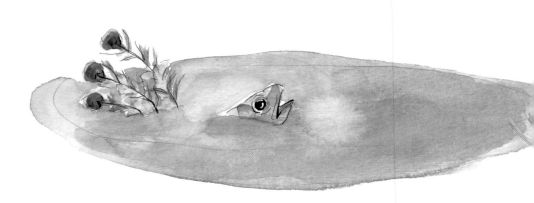

And the porcupine,
between happy somersaults
in his borrowed wool,
was admiring the lovely display
of his very own quills
upon the wingless flamingo.
He decided to tumble by
for a closer inspection,
just to be sure
she was wearing them right.

The porcupine rolled to a stop
at the feet of his lanky friend.
Despite her newfound graceful array,
the flamingo was eager to have her wings back.
She began hopping about, gesturing wildly,
trying in vain to attract
the attention of the turtle ...

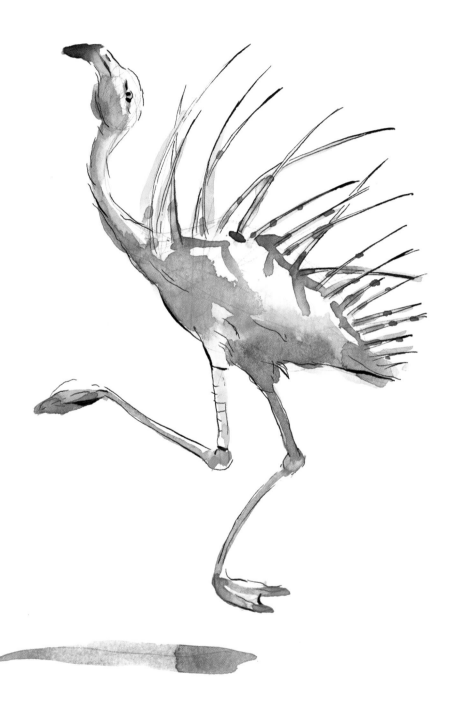